Santa

Trip of Love

(Eldon Wayne Gunter)

Book One of a soon to come Santa series

To My Mrs. Claus

Thank you Judy!

Acknowledgements

This has been a true labor of love for me. Seven years ago, my journey led me to a crimson velvet suit. My love for children and my concern for their everlasting futures allowed it to be a perfect fit! Without my Loving Heavenly Father, His Son and Holy Spirit this would not have been possible!

Since many hands make work light, I wanted to take a moment and give my thanks to those who played a vital role in this endeavor.

Addison, Natalie, and Graysen, I just loved your illustrations and couldn't wait to see them in the book!

Andrew & Ali and Alexandra, you all inspire me daily, thank you for being such wonderful grandchildren! (P.S. Andrew and Ali I can't wait to see the great grandchild)

Lynell and Ron, thank you for your support and encouragement!

Norma, thank for your editing skills and helpful suggestions!

Thank you Amazon and CreateSpace for making this so easy to do!

THANK YOU TO ALL THE WONDERFUL CHILDREN THAT HAVE CROSSED MY PATH AS SANTA...........YES, THIS MEANS YOU TOO!

Contents

The Beginning

Once upon a time, deep in the region of the North Pole, a man with a snow white beard was fast asleep. He was jolly and round; a man who was very popular with all of the townspeople. Every year he would invite all his friends and family to a large celebration.

This little town was a very special town because all of the townspeople were physically similar to the bearded fellow. We call them elves.

The bearded man and his wife were only slightly larger than the rest of the folks in town, about a head taller, in fact. They were always sharing their home and food with anyone who was in need. Mrs. Claus was a wonderful cook—yes, their last name is Claus—and she provided all the goodies for their yearly celebration. Mr. Claus loved to make toys for all the children in the town and he employed several of the townspeople to help. He was a master toy maker and his shop grew and grew each year. It was hard to find enough elves to help make all the toys.

This night, as he was fast asleep, an angel appeared to him in a dream. The angel told him that God was very pleased with all their good works and with how all the people of the town loved each other. The angel told him that God loved all people. In fact, God loved them so much that he wanted Mr. Claus to consider traveling around the world, sharing with all children the same way he did in his own town. The angel said God would be very pleased if Mr. Claus would share his love with all the world's children.

The next morning, when he awoke, he told Mrs. Claus what he had dreamed. He was very confused and was sure he would not be able to handle such a large task. Mrs. Claus suggested that he pray humbly and, in doing so, ask God to show him how he could possibly achieve such an undertaking. So, immediately he and his wife went to his quiet place and fell down on their knees to ask God to make them aware of how they could accomplish such a huge feat.

When they arose, Mr. Claus had a glow on his face and a twinkle in his eyes. He told his wife that God had indeed shown him how to do what God asked of him. God had assured him that he would guide Mr. Claus all the way and never let him be alone.

After much more prayer, Mr. Claus and his wife sat down and laid out the plans as they felt God directing them. Mrs. Claus even suggested that since Mr. Claus's favorite color was red she could make him a red suit and hat. She told him that red stands for the blood of Christ that was shed for all. She said she could add white trim, which would display Christ's purity.

She also suggested that as he would be traveling all over the world, he would need a name that would span the continents; a name that would ring out a feeling of being loved in the hearts of families for years and years to come. So, she organized a contest, asking the townspeople to suggest and decide upon a name to call Mr. Claus. They offered a big prize for the final name that was picked.

The people began sending in their suggestions and the list grew and grew. Some of the names submitted were The Large One, Big Boy, Jelly Belly, White Beard, and The Red Giver. After a week or so they were ready to declare a winner. Finally they picked the name *Santa*. Since their last name was Claus, he became known as *Santa Claus*.

Santa then invited all the people to kneel and give praise to God for allowing him to glorify God in such a wonderful display of love. Mr. and Mrs. Claus also thanked everyone for joining together in the sharing of their talents and gifts for the purpose of making a time for the children of the world to feel a special love relationship—a relationship that would show the love God shared when he offered his Son, Jesus, as the ultimate gift for everyone. Children would receive a gift, unearned by them, as a display of love from a gracious giver. All the children had to do was accept the gift.

Santa's Workshop and the Reindeer

Santa Claus needed to build a huge workshop that would handle all the materials needed to make all the toys for the boys and girls of the world. He would have to hire a lot of workers for year-round service to keep up with the population growth of the world. Santa also needed a headman to oversee the workers. His first thought was of a young man that he knew was a man of God and for whom everyone had great respect. His name was Buddy, and when Santa approached him about this important position, Buddy's eyes lit up and tears ran down his cheeks. He was so happy that Santa had so much confidence in him.

Buddy began hiring workers and proved to be a wonderful servant leader. He selected team captains and let each of them select their helpers. As time passed, everyone was cross-trained for all departments. This allowed them to stay on track and on schedule even when absences occurred.

Santa and Mrs. Claus were very busy with maps and planning routes to cover the world. But they felt something was missing. Santa couldn't walk or run around the world. He fell to his knees and asked God to lead him to a solution. Without hesitation, God gave Santa a way to accomplish this task. God, having also made the world and everything in it, told Santa of a simple solution. Santa was told to build a large sleigh with enough room to carry toys and gifts for each continent. That would allow him to travel back to the North Pole to reload in between continental jaunts. With God's help, Santa would be able to deliver all the toys in one night.

Santa was also charged with finding animals that he felt he could trust to work with him and yet be very gentle with the precious cargo on their many trips. God placed it upon Santa's heart to check out the reindeer of the region. When God created reindeer, he gave them the ability to fly and equipped them with a great sense of direction so they would never get lost—an inner GPS, if you will.

Santa gave thanks once more and proceeded to seek out the reindeer. He called on Buddy and several of the department heads. Santa told them what God had told him, and they headed out to find the specially anointed reindeer. They traveled for several days before they came upon a herd of beautiful white reindeer. Each team captain was told to choose and name one reindeer. The first was Buddy and he named his reindeer Dasher. The next elf named his reindeer Dancer. The third elf named his reindeer Prancer. The fourth elf chose Vixen for his reindeer's name. The fifth elf called his reindeer Comet. The sixth elf named his reindeer Cupid. The seventh elf called his reindeer Donner, and the eighth elf named his Blitzen.

Upon returning home, the tired travelers were greeted by all the townspeople with loud cheers and a huge feast. When all were seated, Santa offered a prayer of thanksgiving, giving God all the praise and glory for leading them to find the reindeer. He also thanked God for choosing them to be part of making all the children of the world happy on a day that would later be named Christmas Day.

Santa's Sleigh and a Crisis

One day, Santa met with the head carpentry elf. Santa shared his plans for a sleigh.

"Wow!" the elf said. "Do you think eight reindeer can pull such a big sleigh?"

"If they need help," Santa said jokingly, "I will call on you and the other elves to help pull it!"

They knew they needed to pray, seeking God's blessing over this project. So they knelt and prayed for guidance.

Work days in Santa's Workshop were long and hard. Everything had gone as planned, until some of the lumber had gotten wet and was taking much too long to dry out. Santa called all the elves together, and they decided to cut more trees and take the logs to the sawmill for cutting into dry lumber. This took better than two weeks, and time was slipping away.

Santa hired more workers to help speed up the work. Once all the lumber was delivered, they began building. They steadily made up some of the lost time. Santa was such a God-focused person, the elves worked even harder to please God. After two weeks they were ready to paint the new sleigh and could not decide on a color. One elf said, "Let's paint it blue like the sky." Another said to paint it green like the trees and grass. Still another elf said to paint it black like the night. One elf even suggested yellow for the sun. Santa was so proud of them because all the colors that were suggested were colors of God's creation. Mrs. Claus told them to paint the sleigh as red as Santa's suit and hat so it would remind all of the cost of God's gift that he had given to all people.

After the sleigh had been finished, the elves gathered the reindeer together for a trial run. Santa and Buddy strapped themselves in and cheers rang out from all the elves, saying, "Glory to God in the highest!" After several flybys, Santa and Buddy came in for a landing and all the townspeople surrounded them. Santa told the elves that he was so excited for them and for the children of the world.

Santa then reminded the elves that the real work was just beginning. They needed to set a date for the big day and decide what they would call it. Buddy spoke up and said, "We should call it Christ's day because God's gift, Christ, is the reason for the day." Mrs. Claus suggested that since this day would involve masses of people, "we should call it Christmas." They all cheered and said, "Amen, amen, amen." Now that they had a name for this day of giving, they needed a special date. After a vote, they all agreed on December 25.

The day had been long and everyone was tired. Santa thanked all of them for the work they had done and said, "Let's call it a day and get some rest, because tomorrow we have a lot of preparation to do."

✳ ✳ ✳ ✳ ✳

Not long after, as Christmas drew ever closer, Santa was having a difficult time. The fog was so thick one day, he was fearful that he would not be able to travel in these conditions. As he and Buddy, his head elf, struggled to come up with a solution, one of the young elves came to them and said he had seen a large reindeer in the woods with a big, bright red nose. "As the reindeer walked along in the darkness, his nose lit up and you could see as clear as day," the elf described.

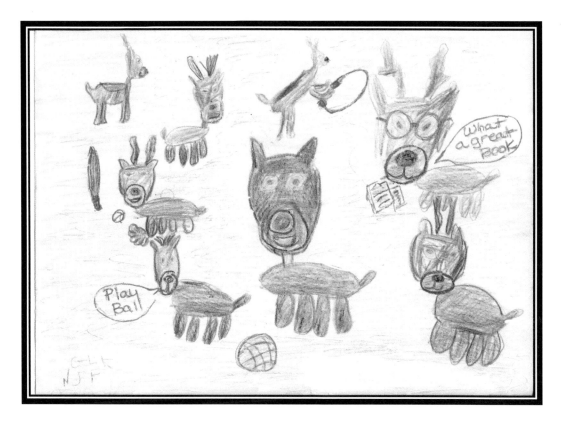

Santa said, "I must see this." They walked into the woods, and then they saw him! He was a handsome reindeer with a huge red nose.

"Please show us how your nose lights up," Santa said.

"Wow!" Santa exclaimed when the reindeer's nose lit up. It was so bright you could see for miles.

"I told you so," the young elf said.

Santa asked the reindeer if he would like to work for him.

"Will I get plenty to eat?"

"Yes, I will feed you very well."

Santa took the new reindeer to meet the other reindeer. They were not too friendly until he showed them what he could do with his nose. Santa asked the eight reindeer to give him a name. They huddled around and agreed to call him Rudolph, the red-nosed reindeer.

Snowed In!

One early morning, snow blanketed the town with three feet of snow. Although the elves were used to a lot of snow, this time was a different story. Santa was depending on their help to get all the toys ready for the big night. Santa had just gotten up and was having a cup of coffee, when he heard a knock on the door. Mrs. Claus opened the door and there stood Buddy, Santa's head elf.

"What are you doing up so early, Buddy? Would you like to join us for a cup of coffee on this cold morning?" Mrs. Claus asked.

"No, thanks," Buddy replied.

Just then Santa heard Buddy's voice and called for him to come in.

Buddy said, "Santa, we have a problem this morning. The town is snowed in and I am the only one that could get out. What are we going to do?"

"Buddy," Santa said, "sit down and we will work out a plan. You know God would never give us a stumbling block without a solution to the problem."

"Santa, how can you be so calm and optimistic at a time like this?"

"You must have faith, Buddy. Remember God places obstacles before us and we must use the brains he gave us to solve our problems. We will just have to find a way to help our friends out of this situation. First, we must call on the reindeer for assistance. They are used to this kind of weather. You go and get Andy and his brother Toby, then get Ralph and his twin Seth. After you get them, bring the reindeer here so we can hook them to the sleigh. If you see anyone else, bring them along to help. We must never give up, because God is in control and will never fail us."

Buddy left quickly to do as Santa directed. He found Andy, Toby, Ralph, and Seth. They then hurried out to gather the reindeer and bring them back to Santa.

An hour later, Buddy and his friends delivered the eight reindeer to Santa's house. Santa was dressed and ready to harness the reindeer to the sleigh. When they were ready, Santa told Mrs. Claus that he and Buddy would be gone for a while and not to worry.

Off they went toward the little town to dig their friends out of the deep snow. When they arrived, some of the folk had already dug out and were helping their neighbors dig out. It was good to see them helping one another. As Santa approached, several men told him that they were ready to get back to work on the toys. Alvin, the spokesman, said that time was going fast and they only had two months to make all the toys that were needed for Christmas. Santa told him he had opened several thousand letters from children and Mrs. Claus was putting their requests in order for each continent.

"I don't know what I would do without Mrs. Claus. She is so organized. It surely makes my work so much easier when everything is in order. I have gotten so many special requests from all over the world that I need to hire more workers to help open the mail and help Mrs. Claus separate the mail. She works so hard and never complains."

After the town was dug out, the elves could get to the workshop, and it was soon buzzing with activity again.

"We gave the reindeer a workout today. We used them to take loads of tired workers home and then pick up fresh and rested workers delivering them to the workshop. I hope any more snow holds off for a while so we can catch up on all the work," Santa told Mrs. Claus.

After the long day of helping the townspeople clear the snow away from their homes, Santa was tuckered out. He said good night to everyone and went straight to bed. Mrs. Claus had to keep poking Santa through the night because of his loud snoring. She knew he was completely worn out, for he usually never snored much. She got little sleep that night.

When Santa woke the next morning, Mrs. Claus was still fast asleep. He let her stay asleep and made coffee and breakfast himself. It was not nearly as good as good as hers!

Troubles at Santa's Workshop

As Santa was finishing his breakfast one morning, he heard a knock at the door. By the way the person pounded on the door, someone was in a hurry to get in.

"Come in," Santa said.

As the door opened, Santa was surprised to see Buddy and Joe, two of Santa's elves, standing there with worried looks on their faces.

"What's wrong?"

"Santa, we have a major problem. The motor that runs the conveyor for the entire workshop has shut down. We don't have a replacement for it. That means the whole system is shut down. What are we going to do? We only have three weeks to finish the toys. Oh, Santa, what are we going to do?"

Santa suggested they check with the townspeople. They did and one elderly man came forward.

"Santa, I would like to give it a shot. You know, I was one of the best electricians in my company."

Santa agreed and asked the man to go to the workshop. "Good luck," he added.

After many hours of trial and error, the man got the motor running again. Santa smiled and said, "I knew you would get us going."

All the elves in the workshop applauded, cheered, and sang, "For he's a jolly good fellow!"

Santa told everyone to go back to work, and keep an eye on that motor. "You just have to have a little faith," he said.

As the day progressed, everything seemed to be working well. "We lost some precious time, and we must try to make it up by giving our all for the next several days," Santa told his workers. "I will not let God down. He gave me a very big job and I will not disappoint him."

A few days passed and things seemed to be on schedule. Santa was very pleased.

Just as he was feeling that everything was going well, Buddy came in and told Santa, "We have another problem. Prancer seems to think he should be in the lead instead of Dancer. He's acting very badly. I have talked to him but he wants to see you. If you let him change places, Dasher will be upset and I think the others will side with him. I don't know how we are going to handle this one."

Santa agreed to see if he could settle the dispute.

He approached the reindeer and told them they could not be unhappy this close to Christmas. "Prancer, why do you feel that you should be the one in front?"

"Santa, I feel sad not leading because I think I'm bigger and stronger, and I'm better looking," Prancer confidently replied.

"Do you realize," Santa asked, "that the reindeer in that position is responsible for leading us around the world in one night? Dasher has agreed to take that responsibility. Are you willing to accept it?"

Prancer lowered his head and said, "No."

"Good," said Santa. "Each one of you is just as important as the others. I need you all or we cannot complete this task that God has placed with us. Let's make this first Christmas the very best."

When Santa returned to the workshop, he found more and more letters from children telling him what they wanted for Christmas. The elves were getting worried about not being finished in time, and now they had to add to their production. Santa had a big surprise for Buddy and the elves. He unlocked and opened a big door at the back of the workshop. When they saw what was in that room, the elves were overjoyed. Santa had been gathering toys for backup. Santa had saved the day!

Santa's First Trip

Santa Claus had spent many nights planning his trips and deciding how much time he would be able to spend on each continent. "Since Asia has the most people," he exclaimed, "I will plan for them to be first. The second continent will be Africa, then North America and Europe. Next I will go to South America and Australia. The last will be Antarctica." He had worked out the routes so he could make the best time. "I had better get some sleep so I can be fresh and alert tomorrow, the biggest day of my life."

The next morning Santa awoke to a lot of noise outside his window. Buddy had the sleigh loaded, the reindeer harnessed, and ten helpers ready to go. Santa quickly drank a cup of coffee to wake himself up, ate a nutritious breakfast, and walked outside. He thanked his helpers for all the effort they had put forth for one of the most wonderful days of the year. He asked everyone to kneel and thank God for his goodness and mercy. Santa also thanked God for sending his Son, Jesus, to save the world. Jesus' birth was celebrated on December 25 every year, and Santa was so glad they had picked that date for giving children gifts.

Santa climbed up on the sleigh, along with his ten helpers. With a loud voice, he called out each reindeer's name: "On Dasher, on Dancer, on Prancer, and Vixen; on Comet, on Cupid, on Donner and Blitzen!" And away they did fly.

On the way, Santa gave instructions to his helpers for when they arrived at each home. "When we stop, be as quiet as possible. We don't want to wake up the children. If you find anyone awake, use the twilight dust we made and they will fall fast asleep."

One of his helpers asked Santa if the dust could harm anyone. "No," Santa answered, "because this came from God. He knew we would need something to help children fall asleep."

All went well in Asia, and they were making good time; in fact, faster than Santa had figured they would. So, off they headed to the North Pole for their second load. Buddy was waiting for him and his workers were ready to load the sleigh again.

After the sleigh was loaded for the second time, Santa was off to Africa. "This trip may take a little longer," Santa reported, "so everyone must work fast."

One of the helpers developed a toothache and could not get any relief. Santa had to use some twilight dust to let him sleep until the dentist could pull his tooth.

The sky was clear, but the temperature had dropped about twenty degrees. The helpers were beginning to feel very cold. They didn't want to complain, however, because Santa might give their job to someone else.

"We're almost there," Santa announced, "so get everything ready. Remember, not a lot of noise; we do not want to wake the children."

The job was done so fast they couldn't believe they were ready to return for another load of toys. Away they flew to the North Pole. When they were loaded again, they flew to North America. One of the helpers said, "Santa, could we please stop and see the United States? We have heard so much about it. I understand there are many Christians there, like us."

"Yes, that's right," Santa said. "It's hard to be a Christian when there are so many sinful things around. I'm glad we all are Christians and not faced with sin in our town."

So, another continent was completed.

"Let's head home for another load. The next continent is Europe. We need to really watch the children. The last trip I saw several children pretending to be asleep when they weren't. Use your twilight dust if you feel a child is not asleep."

After Europe, the next continent they flew to was South America. "We are running right on schedule," Santa reported, "but we have two more continents after this one. I would like to finish before daylight and get a few hours' sleep."

They left South America and returned to the North Pole to load up one last time. "This time we will take toys for both Australia and Antarctica. This will save us a lot of time."
The trip was long, because Australia was "down under," as they say.

Everything went well on this trip until they got to Antarctica where they ran into a huge snow storm. The reindeer were doing a super job and following instructions very well. They almost turned over once due to strong winds. Everyone held on tight until they had cleared the rough weather.

Soon they were ready to go home, their mission completed. Santa reported, "I knew God was in control and gave us traveling mercies for following his commands. I have had wonderful assistants to help me with so huge a task."

The Day After Christmas

All the townspeople were outside, waiting for the sleigh to return home. When Santa's sleigh landed, the people cheered. Santa told them to go home to rest for a while. Santa told them he had a big surprise for them the next morning.

The townspeople and all the workers were invited to the workshop for the surprise. As they gathered around the big Christmas tree in the center of the workshop, they found tables filled with all kinds of food from all over the world. "Since we flew through the whole world last night, I thought it would be nice to sample food from each continent. You can taste Chinese food, Mexican food, German food, and more from every country in the world."

When everyone was seated, Santa gave thanks to God for all his goodness and for giving them a safe trip to share gifts with the children of the world just as the wise men had brought gifts to the Christ Child.

After the prayer, they sampled all types of food. When they were full, Santa told them he had another surprise for them. He went to a secret room and unlocked the double doors. Santa asked Buddy and his department heads to do the honor and open the doors wide. Inside were gifts for all the townspeople! Everything that anyone could imagine was there.

All the people shouted, "Thank you, Santa!" When they had opened their gifts, Santa told them to take a couple of days off to rest, "because we must start the new year planning for next Christmas."

❄ ❄ ❄ ❄ ❄

Santa prayed to God that night: "Did we do this large task in accordance to your will? We worked very hard and everyone knew we were doing this for our Lord and Savior. We just wanted to know if you are pleased."

Santa went off to bed and was asleep in a short time. The angel who had appeared to him earlier returned in a dream and answered Santa's question. "Santa, God is so very proud of you and all who worked so hard to establish a time for all the earth to see that He is thinking of His children. When he sent His only Son, God needed a time of the year to remind everyone who Jesus is and why he was sent to the earth. You have just taken care of establishing that day. This is your gift to God."

When Santa awoke the next morning, Mrs. Claus saw the glow in his face and asked him why he was so happy.

"I was visited by the angel last night and was told that God is very pleased with what we accomplished for Him. You, too, had a large part in this. Thanks, and I love you."

After the first of the year, Santa called a meeting with Buddy, his head elf, and all who had helped him. "We have established a new holiday. We have made history. So we must start planning for next Christmas."

Then Santa thanked all the townspeople for helping him establish the first Christmas to celebrate the birth of our Savior. "All the world will understand that I am just a part of the ongoing story of how God sent his Son to be born and to die for all of us. His birth will be celebrated every year until he returns to take us home."

❄ ❄ ❄ ❄ ❄

So, as we celebrate Jesus' birth, may the whole world soon come to know Him as their personal Savior. Amen.

Santa
Book One
Trip of Love

Eldon Wayne Gunter

Made in the USA
Charleston, SC
01 December 2013